For my son Oliver, with love

First published in Great Britain 1985
by Methuen Children's Books
11 New Fetter Lane, London EC4P 4EE
Copyright © 1985 by Heather S Buchanan
Printed in Great Britain
by W. S. Cowell Ltd, Ipswich

ISBN 0 416 48550 2

Matilda Mouse's
Patchwork Life-jackets

Heather S. Buchanan

Methuen Children's Books

Winter was coming and Matilda Mouse was getting ready for the cold days and nights with her family. She lived with her parents and twin baby brothers, Humphrey and Oliver, in a cottage.

Their home was in a beautiful Chinese teapot on a mantelpiece. It was cracked and had lost its lid, but was so pretty it couldn't be thrown away, and it made a perfect house for the mice.

An old lady also lived in the cottage, with a tabby cat called Harriet who always seemed to be hungry.

Matilda used to sit behind the spout of the teapot in the shadows, watching everything that went on in the cottage.

One day, the lady brought out a sewing basket and began cutting material of all shapes and colours into squares. Then she began sewing them together again to make a pattern. Matilda thought this was a very strange thing to do, but when it was finished, she had made it into a beautiful patchwork apron.

Matilda crept back into the teapot. She had had a wonderful idea. The twins were so alike that she could hardly tell them apart, but if she made them each a different patchwork jacket, she would know which twin was which.

That night, when the twins were going to bed, Matilda's father lit the candle stub which stood in the middle of the teapot. The light could barely be seen from outside, but just to be safe, they waited until the bed upstairs creaked as the old lady climbed into it.

Matilda went down to the kitchen table and squeezed inside the sewing-basket, past the scissors and the thimble, until she reached the needle case.

Using all her strength she pulled out a shiny, silver needle, then unwound some thread from a cotton reel and wrapped it round her middle. She tucked the needle through this, like a sword, and climbed slowly back up to the teapot.

Matilda's father hauled in the needle and cotton, and she went back to get some material. She chose different coloured bits for each jacket and tied them onto her head with a piece of cotton. Then she spotted some cotton wool, and tied that on too.

Matilda had been watching out for the cat, but she was in no danger because Harriet had gone out to hunt for field mice in the garden.

Back in the teapot house, the twins had woken up, and Matilda's parents had gone out to find some supper. Matilda spread out her material and told the twins about their jackets.

They helped to nibble the material into the right shape for sewing together again and then jumped up and down on the cotton wool to make it flat and wide like pastry for a pie. Matilda bit the cotton wool to the same size as each jacket and sewed it inside the lining.

Matilda stitched hard for a long time. At last the patchwork jackets were ready for the twins to try on, but they still needed some tiny buttons.

'Stay here and be good,' she told the twins. 'I'll soon be back.'

Once in the sewing basket again, she waded about in a sea of shiny buttons in the button box. She was so busy choosing which to have, that she didn't see Harriet come softly in and look up at the teapot on the mantelpiece.

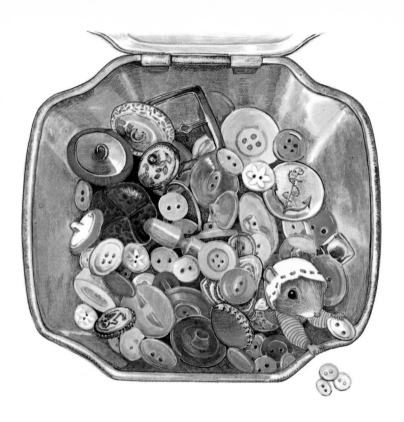

When at last Matilda was satisfied with her choice of buttons and turned for home, she saw a dreadful sight. The naughty twins had climbed out of the teapot and were sitting on top of the spout, and Harriet was making her way slowly but surely towards them.

Suddenly, Humphrey scuttled back inside but Oliver was still hovering at the top. Harriet sprang up on to the mantelpiece, sending a plate crashing to the ground. A paw flashed out and caught the little mouse.

There was a frightful tearing noise. Matilda couldn't bear to look. But Oliver was safely inside the teapot again, and Harriet was left spitting and growling, with cotton wool and yellow material stuck to her claws.

Matilda hid behind the sewing basket, shaking with fright. But the crash from the broken plate had woken the old lady. She came downstairs, put the cat out of the window, closed it firmly and went back up to bed again.

Matilda crept back home. The twins were holding each other tightly and crying. She hugged them close, and sighed with relief. Oliver's jacket was badly torn across the back where Harriet's claw had ripped it, but Matilda knew that if he hadn't been wearing it, the cat would certainly have caught him. Her patchwork jacket had saved the little mouse's life.

Matilda decided there and then that they must *all* have jackets – a beautiful flowery one for her mother, smart stripes and checks for her father, and lots of different shapes on her own.

A few days later her father brought home a long piece of satin ribbon which made smart ties for the front of each jacket.

Now the mice were warm all winter through, but, best of all, they were safe from Harriet the cat!